Puffin

GW00858147

Against

A nine-year-old girl whose non-stop chatter rids the town of aliens; a disastrous competition between two master chefs; a genie who makes more than magic; a little girl who sees the sky for the first time; and a pocket-sized visitor who gives the gift of confidence to a shy boy.

Sound weird? Strange things happen all the time! Here's an irresistible collection of extremely unlikely stories by one of Australia's favourite children's authors.

LIA REUTENS

OTHER PUFFIN TITLES BY ROBIN KLEIN

Hating Alison Ashley
Halfway Across the Galaxy and Turn Left
People Might Hear You
Games . . .
I Shot An Arrow (Picture Puffin)
Boss of the Pool

Against the Odds

Illustrated by Bill Wood

ROBIN KLEIN

LIA REUTENS

Puffin Books

Puffin Books
Penguin Books Australia Ltd
487 Maroondah Highway, PO Box 257
Ringwood, Victoria, 3134, Australia
Penguin Books Ltd
Harmondsworth, Middlesex, England
Viking Penguin Inc.
40 West 23rd Street, New York, NY 10010, USA
Penguin Books Canada Limited
2801 John Street, Markham, Ontario, Canada, L3R 1B4
Penguin Books (N.Z.) Ltd
182-190 Wairau Road, Auckland 10, New Zealand

First published by Viking Kestrel, 1989
Published in Puffin, 1989
Copyright © Robin Klein, 1989
Illustrations Copyright © Bill Wood, 1989

Typeset in Plantin Roman by Leader Composition
Made and printed in Australia by Australian Print Group

CIP

Klein, Robin, 1936-
Against all odds.

ISBN 0 14 032705 3.

1. Children's stories, Australian. I. Wood, Bill. II.
Title.
A823'.3

CONTENTS

Chouls	1
The Two Chefs	29
How Nellie Patch Saved the Little Town of Sycamore	41
Glumly	51
Zarab-Hasaka	73

Chouls

ONE

It was about the size of a hubcap and lay outrageously in the centre of Aunt Moira's neat front lawn. Julian had nimble reflexes from months of always being blamed for any household or garden damage, so he quickly scooped up the object and hid it in his school bag. He wiped his shoes on the rubber doormat which was scrubbed once a week with disinfectant, hung his blazer meticulously on the coat hanger just inside the hall, and stepped into the kitchen. You didn't actually enter any of the rooms in Aunt Moira's house; you stepped into them. Very quietly, very warily.

'You're late!' Aunt Moira sniped without glancing up from polishing one of her hideous brass ornaments. 'I hope you wiped your shoes. I hope you hung up your blazer with all the buttons done up. Wendy said you borrowed her coloured pencils

1

without asking. Just for that you can take both the rubbish bins out tonight. You left a dab of toothpaste in the basin this morning. I just polished the banister with Marvel Oak. Don't you dare touch it when you go upstairs.'

'Hi there, Julian!' he said mutely to himself. 'How was school today? I've just made a pot of tea and some nice hot scones. Let's take them into the living room and watch TV together.'

'Don't hang around underfoot,' Aunt Moira barked. 'You go and do your homework, young man.'

Julian stepped out of the kitchen and into the hall which was as clean and bleak as an empty butcher shop window. He went upstairs, dutifully not touching the banister. Aunt Moira would one day rub all the patina off with her incessant polishing and sprucing and rubbing. In the six months he'd lived in this house, he felt as though his own layers of skin had been scrubbed raw, leaving all the nerve endings exposed.

His cousin Wendy was in the bathroom on the landing, frizzing up her hair. It looked like a sausage roll plastered across her forehead, but Julian didn't say so. He avoided meeting her eyes in the bathroom mirror. Meeting Wendy's eyes was like trying to outstare a bad-tempered kelpie.

'I told Mum how you pinched my pencils, you squirt!' she crowed. 'You set foot in my room again and I'll tear off your skinny little arms!'

Julian went up the three steps to his room under the roof and shut the door. In that house it was forbidden to sit on any made bed, so he perched on the uncomfortable wooden chair and tackled his homework. It was simpler, anyhow, to do what Aunt Moira demanded and avoid having her attention focused upon you for longer than necessary. When he finished the map of Canada, he stretched and looked down at the back lawn bordered by sharp-edged rocks. It was unpleasantly like a leaf of cabbage being munched by spiky teeth. In its centre was a concrete birdbath to which no birds came. Aunt Moira wouldn't allow it to be filled with water because she claimed mosquitoes would breed there. It was a beastly garden and not worth looking at.

Julian remembered the hubcap and pulled it from his school bag with one ear nervously to the door. Wendy felt free to burst into his room any old time. If she saw the hubcap, she'd probably accuse him of stealing it, and she'd call Aunt Moira. They'd both stand there, not exactly glowing with triumph, for they weren't capable of glowing about anything, but staring beadily at him with pleased, smug faces, because they'd found something positive to criticize.

It was a strange hubcap, unlike any he'd seen before, beautifully made with intricate seams and an indented pattern of numbers etched around the rim. He flipped it over to look at the back, then dropped it, startled, on the bed. It had started to hum, a faint whirring sound, not much louder than a bee reeling from one clover head to another. The humming, if indeed there had been any outside his imagination, was smothered by Wendy bawling up the stairs, 'Mum said to tell you there's a tin of macaroni cheese you can heat up for your dinner. We're going down to the shops to buy me some new jeans and don't forget to wash out the saucepan either, you little nerd.'

Julian absently heard them leave. Usually it was a joy when they went out and left him alone in the house, but at the moment he was more interested in discovering the source of the mysterious humming. He noticed a smear of oil on the coverlet and he'd never hear the end of that, but he slid his metal ruler under a seam and prised upwards. The top half of the hubcap came off with a snap and something darted out and fastened upon his wrist like a hornet.

Julian stared down at the hornet, which wasn't one at all. It was a tiny lady, no taller than a toothbrush, wearing a natty silver tracksuit and silver high-heeled boots. She was yelling at him in a small shrill voice, and seemed to have a very fluent vocabulary, even if he couldn't understand one word of it.

'I'm sorry!' he said hastily, rubbing at the minute teeth marks on his wrist. 'I didn't know anyone was inside.'

The lady shook her fist furiously, then ran about his bedspread trying to replace the hubcap lid. Julian, contrite about any damage he'd caused, would have helped, but was rather scared of the fierce little lady. He looked inside the hubcap. It was fashioned like a miniature campervan, with a bunk and cabinets, though most of the walls were covered with electronic switches. Before he had a chance to have a really good look, the lid finally slid back into place on some complicated inter-locking system of tabs and hinges. The owner folded her arms grimly and glared from the little slick of spilled oil up at Julian.

'I really am sorry. Have I broken something? There are some tools out in the garden shed and I'll fix anything I've damaged,' Julian said, though he felt sick at the thought of going into Uncle Ralph's toolshed without permission. Uncle Ralph was just like Aunt Moira, only larger and meaner. The panicky feeling churned about in his stomach, and he remembered that he hadn't had anything to eat since lunch time at school, and that had only been a thin sandwich with a filling of pallid cheese. In his bag there was a chocolate bar which the school librarian had given him for helping to tidy the shelves. It was hoarded for emergencies, but he guessed that this qualified as one. He politely broke a corner from the chocolate bar and held it out. The cross little lady took it rather ungraciously, but seemed to like the taste,

5

because she stopped scowling quite so much and said something to him. It was like being addressed by a butterfly, and Julian had to bend his head to hear, but still couldn't understand her language. He shook his head helplessly.

She felt in her pocket and brought out something metallic that unfolded to the size of a biscuit and gave it to him. The surface was covered with small but visible moving print composed apparently of squiggles. Julian couldn't make any sense of their meaning, but found a little winding knob on one side. The squiggles jumped about and changed to the script of some unknown alphabet, but as he kept turning the knob, the screen eventually became filled with letters he could understand:

My name is space commander Aldorado fully licensed top grade supreme countless decorations and distinctions and that's putting it mildly pal been there done that private lessons given but don't call me I'll call you if there's one thing I can't stand it's starry-eyed amateurs wanting navigation lessons specially big galoopy giants don't give me any more hassles or you'll regret it I've got the best teeth on Polaris 13 you've gone and busted my launching fuel link you thumping great article P.S. You're so clumsy you must need chouls. P.P.S. You can call me Addie for short over and out.

Julian wasn't sure what 'chouls' meant, but he could hardly believe that this fabulous thing had happened to HIM, Julian Shelten, aged eleven, undersized and looking about two years younger than he actually was and no one ever let him forget it, specially Wendy. And here he was entertaining a visiting space commander top grade supreme! He wished he had a posh business card to show her, but all he could manage was the label on the cover of his school folder which said, 'Julian Shelten, Year 6A, West Braythwaite Primary School, Braythwaite.' Addie read it and nodded.

Julian is a soppy name you should change it to something more spunky like Yabros or

7

Grimbolt offer of tools acknowledged but not necessary what I need urgently is a few drops of RMBZ33 to replace what's leaked from the fuel link please fetch pronto though will have to give you an I.O.U. My pay cheque was late again this week (last time I'll ever work for that uncool untogether charter company on sub-Polaris 99!) P.S. You have my word as a commander top grade supreme I'll pay you back next trip here signing off Addie.

'I don't know if we have any RMBZ33 in the toolshed,' Julian said doubtfully. 'There's petrol for the lawn mower and maybe that'll do. I'll get it . . .' He was going to say 'right now' but then thought of taking the key from its hook in the laundry, going down the back path and unlocking the toolshed. The idea made him gulp with fright. 'I'll get it . . . after we have dinner,' he said instead. 'You must be hungry after your long trip from wherever you said you came from, and a little bit of chocolate's not really a balanced diet.'

He went downstairs to the kitchen and prepared the macaroni cheese with more care than usual, even adding some chopped parsley as a garnish. When it was ready he put a few strands into a tiny crystal liqueur glass, because it was the smallest and most elegant container he could find. He took the food back upstairs, even though he wasn't allowed to eat in his room. Addie ate the macaroni

8

cheese suspiciously, but asked for a whole lot more. For such a miniature person, she had a very healthy appetite. Julian hoped she'd forget about his promise to look for fuel, but as soon as she finished eating, she started hectoring him about it through the little metal communication screen.

I've got no time to waste not like some lazy people I could mention I need that RMBZ33 right now there's always a million and one things to do before linking up with an orbital blink my hair's a perfect fright so I've got to fit in a shampoo and set somehow too I'm not going off into orbit looking like a neutron regards from Addie P.S. I'll never even get to first base if you don't hurry yourself you ploddy great giant!

It felt weird being bossed around by someone only a few centimetres in height, but the little green letters on the screen kept flashing relentlessly up and down like a migraine. Julian tried to remember exactly where Uncle Ralph kept the plastic container of petrol for the lawn mower. He fancied it was on a ledge behind the jars of nuts and bolts, all graded according to size. Uncle Ralph's toolshed was really just an awe-inspiring extension of the house, and Julian was alarmed by both.

'It's sort of complicated getting into the toolshed,' he said. 'The things there aren't really mine. I'll get into a lot of trouble if I'm caught.'

What on earth can there be to scare a big clump like you quit making dumb giant jokes let's get this show on the airways I'd better come with you to make sure it's proper RMBZ33 and not some other low-grade rubbish seeing you obviously need chouls move it Buster!

'I think you should get into my pocket, then,' Julian said. 'Otherwise I might accidently step on you.'

You'd soon hear about it if you did!

'And if I carried you in my hand I might trip and drop you. It would be a long way to fall. By the way, what are 'chouls'?'

I know how to crash-land go teach your grandmother chouls are those things people with bad eyesight wear can't remember your word for it o.k. I'll travel in your pocket if I must but don't expect me to like it.

Julian took her downstairs and collected the toolshed key with fingers as numb as unthawed fish fillets. Before his courage drained clean away, he hurried along the path and unlocked the shed door. The container was where he'd remembered, on the shelf behind the work bench. 'There!' he said. 'I think I've found you some RMBZ33!'

Addie scrambled from his pocket to the work bench and unscrewed the lid and sniffed. The little screen buzzed angrily.

Who are you trying to kid I didn't come down in the last shower of meteorites this is not a bit like RMBZ33 I wouldn't dream of using this stuff even to zip over to sub-polaris 99 to have my nails done and that trip takes only fifteen seconds you'll have to do a whole lot better giant scram beat it vamoose get lost I'll find some proper RMBZ33 myself thanks for the memories Addie.

She ignored him and inspected all the jars along the shelf, and the little screen flashed prickly jumbled phrases while she was grumbling crossly to herself.

It's surely not asking too much you'd think on this tacky oversized planet they'd have a little bit of spare launching fuel talk about uncivilized get your great mitt out of the way giant I nearly tripped these boots cost two pay packets and if that heel comes loose you'll rue the day!

11

Julian watched as she inspected the bottles of methylated spirits, turpentine and paint stripper. She sniffed at each one and looked increasingly more annoyed.

'I don't think we'll find any,' Julian said apologetically. 'We could go out early tomorrow and look. Maybe unleaded petrol might do. I have a little bit of money saved up, but you'll only need a little bit of fuel. Don't worry, we'll call in at the garage as soon as it opens tomorrow.'

Addie didn't look very convinced and muttered to herself in his pocket all the way up the garden path and into the kitchen. She only shut up when she saw Aunt Moira and Wendy standing triumphantly over the macaroni cheese saucepan Julian had forgotten to wash.

He impulsively pushed Addie's silver helmet down out of sight and buttoned the flap of his shirt pocket before Aunt Moira turned around and saw him.

'So! Lurking around outside, are you, and getting up to no good! The very idea, leaving my good sink cluttered up with filthy dishes like a room in a slum! I suppose you expected poor little Wendy to clean up after you!'

Aunt Moira had bought three different brands of cleaning powders on special and a repulsive copper sailing ship plaque to hang in the living room. Wendy was wearing new jeans and new hair combs and an insufferable now-you're-going-to-get-it expression. Julian nervously approached the sink and filled it with hot water, adding a careful half-lid of detergent because it was advisable to use that amount and no more if Aunt Moira was around. He began to scour the saucepan, uneasily conscious of the slight bulge that was Addie in his shirt pocket.

'I bet I can guess what he was doing outside,' Wendy piped maliciously. 'Probably he's been up and down the back lane shoving over people's rubbish bins.'

Julian didn't say anything, because verbal defence was useless. The best thing was to make yourself very quiet and small and hope that their spitefulness would dissolve in the shortest possible time. Luckily Aunt Moira was anxious to hang up her ghastly new plaque and left the kitchen, but Wendy stayed, ostentatiously sliding the new combs in and out of her fuzzy hair.

'We had dinner at a café,' she gloated. 'I had four jam donuts for dessert, and Mum let me buy a new tape, too, only you needn't bother asking if you can hear it, because I won't let you!'

Julian rinsed the saucepan in cold water and put it in the drying rack, then carefully wiped down the bench top. Aunt Moira carried on like a revolution if you left even a droplet of water on the sink.

'I saw that Luke kid who's in your class,' Wendy said. 'He gave me a message to pass on to you.'

13

Julian's face brightened. He hadn't been able to make friends with anyone at school yet. A playground at recess when you had no friends was the loneliest and most desolate wilderness in the world. Luke would be a good mate to have.

'He said to tell you . . .' Wendy said.

Julian waited hopefully. Maybe Luke had invited him round to his place tomorrow, to go to the soccer club.

'He said to tell you it'll be a waste of time if you turn up for soccer training tomorrow morning,' Wendy said. 'He said you should go Wednesdays instead. Wednesdays is when they have training for the little brats under eight.'

Julian kept his face expressionless so she wouldn't guess at his despair. He went on scrubbing the sink, but saw only his reflection beyond it in the window pane. He and Wendy were almost exactly the same height which was pitiful, because she was eighteen months younger. And her whole aggressive personality was so overpowering, it was as though he came only up to her shoulder, anyhow. He turned to go upstairs.

'Hey, what's that you've got in your pocket?' Wendy demanded.

'It's nothing. It's just . . . my hankie . . .'

Wendy, not believing him, made a greedy, lightning-swift snatch and Addie was hauled out with her silver boots dangling. Addie stayed very still and didn't move a muscle, and Julian could

14

tell by her eyes that she recognized danger and knew how to handle it.

'A Barbie doll!' Wendy hooted incredulously. 'Just wait till I tell everyone at school you play with Barbie dolls! Where did you get it, then, Julian, pinched it from the toy shop? My, isn't she sweet all dressed up in a silver jump suit and a little-bitty silver gloves!'

'You give that back!' Julian said, but Wendy skipped out of the room and ran upstairs and slammed her door. Julian went desperately into the living room and looked at Aunt Moira, who was busy with a measuring tape gauging the exact spot to put her new plaque. The sections of wall on either side of the proposed nail must be mathematically equal, even if it took her all night to work it out.

'Wendy took something of mine and won't give it back,' Julian said.

'Don't you start any fights with Wendy!'

'I never started anything. I had something in my pocket and she grabbed it and took it up to her room.'

'Nonsense. Wendy wouldn't do things like that. You're making it up, and anyhow, even if she did, it would be just some light-hearted little game. She's just high-spirited, that's all, not always sulking and brooding like you. What was it she's supposed to have taken, if anyone could believe your side of things?'

Julian swallowed. 'It was a . . . sort of doll, like a Barbie doll.'

'Talk about selfish! You wouldn't have any use for a little doll you found, so what's the harm in Wendy having it? I don't want to hear another word about it. You go on up to bed.'

But Julian went and listened outside Wendy's door. He could hear her murmuring with satisfaction to herself, 'Oh, what a cute doll! I'll call her Cindy Leigh and tomorrow I'll get Mum to make a pretty little ballet skirt. I wonder if her legs bend right back? She could be a ballerina ornament to go on top of my jewel box. I'll find some glue tomorrow to stick her on, and if that doesn't work, I'll use a stapler.'

Julian looked at the little metal screen in his hand. It flickered incoherently and furiously, making no sense at all. Addie's thoughts were unprintable. Soon Wendy, tired after her shopping expedition, went to bed. Julian allowed fifteen minutes, then stealthily opened her door. She was fast asleep under her frilly quilt like a large pink piglet nestled in straw. He looked about for Addie and found her stuck up on a high shelf with Wendy's vast collection of dolls. Her fierce little eyes glinted with repressed outrage. He picked her up and took her back to his own room.

About time too what took you forever how would you like to be stuck up on a mountain with fat giantesses combing your hair in different styles with a toothbrush ugh I thought you and I were supposed to be working together as a team some team effort huh and blah I was there for a trillion maxihours!!!

'I had to wait till she fell asleep,' Julian explained. 'You don't know what she's like. If she wants something badly enough, or even if she doesn't particularly want it but doesn't want anyone else to have it, she'll just hang on and . . . tug.'

Addie stopped scowling and went rather quiet.

Well I suppose you did your best I'd have bitten her but I'm fussy about what I sink my teeth into now I'm going to shampoo my hair after that sordid toothbrush business and get some sleep this has been a rackety old day and I don't mean maybe goodnight giant signing off Addie.

Julian set his alarm clock for 6 a.m., one hour earlier than the usual time for his paper round, but he didn't want to be in the house when Wendy woke up and discovered her loss. He didn't want Addie to be there, either. Wendy would take his room apart.

Addie wasn't particularly pleased at being woken at such an early hour, but permitted herself to be put in his pocket. Julian also took the spacecraft, which certainly wouldn't be safe in his room once Wendy woke up. He put it in the hessian bag he used for the paper round and set off on his battered old bike, thinking desperately of different types of fuel and how he could obtain a sample of each. It was imperative for Addie to head back to her own planet as soon as possible. This was no place for her, not with people like Wendy who would staple her on to a jewel box as an ornament. Nor with people like Aunt Moira who would probably reach for a can of Mortein or a fly swat if she as much as set eyes on Addie.

He hurried through his round, folding each paper and throwing it accurately to land just inside a porch or verandah. Everyone in this area said he was the best paper boy they'd ever had, because the papers were never left out in the rain. It was a small, trivial thing to be proud about, and one which certainly couldn't be compared with winning decorations for space travel, but when the little communication screen beeped and spelled out, hey you aren't such a bad shot giant! he sat taller on the bike because Addie had noticed his one skill.

After delivering the last paper he went to the garage on Boyd Street and stood uncertainly by the lead-free petrol bowser. He could have saved himself the bother, because the attendant was very scathing about someone without a car wanting to buy a cup full of petrol, unleaded or otherwise.

'How do I know what you want it for, eh?' the man demanded suspiciously. Petrol's dangerous. You could start a fire with it. Clear out, and don't come pestering me again or I'll tell your Uncle Ralph.'

Julian rode away, defeated, and went aimlessly down to the lake in the park. He sat on the concrete bank and took Addie out of his pocket so that she could have a change of scenery. She didn't seem to be in the mood to appreciate scenery, though. Julian guessed that she was depressed about the prospect of having to live indefinitely on a strange planet where nothing was her size. He knew how she felt. It would be the same feeling that had swamped him when he'd had to come and live at Aunt Moira's. A sort of exile.

'I'm sorry about that garage business,' he said.

Never mind no point in having a conniption about it I don't think their stuff was the right kind of fuel anyhow it just didn't smell right.

'To tell the truth, I don't even know where to start looking for RMBZ33,' Julian confessed. 'The only thing I can think of is to take some of what's left in your fuel tank to a chemist and ask them to analyse it and have some made up specially. But it would probably be very expensive and you'd have to wait till I saved up enough money from my paper round. That might take months.'

Forget about months if I don't get launched in the next ten minutes I'll miss the orbital blink anyway oh well nothing for it but to wait for the next one fancy having to hang around on this great whacky planet waiting for the next O blatherdash!

'When will the next orbital blink come around?' Julian asked. He might, with a bit of luck, be able to hide her in the toolshed till tomorrow, but then she'd have to be moved again, because Uncle Ralph would be home. The bare, neat garden was no good. His room was useless because of Wendy, and nowhere in the house was there one corner safe from Aunt Moira's vacuuming and polishing and gimlet eyes. 'How long before the next orbital blink, Addie?' he asked worriedly.

Don't you know anything two hundred and fifty-seven years of course.

'Two hundred and fifty-seven years?' Julian cried, wondering who would look after her when he'd gone. But because he didn't want to worry her about that, he said as casually as he could, 'Well then, we'll just have to manage. We can bury the spacecraft somewhere in the park and dig it up when you need it, because we're sure to find some RMBZ33 in two hundred and fifty-seven years. I'll be a chemist when I leave school and make some RMBZ33 specially. And it mightn't be so bad living in my pocket. I won't let Wendy snatch you again and I'll talk to you every chance I get so you won't feel too lonely.'

I'm sure you mean well but I'm not used to living in people's pockets back home on Polaris 13 I have a very classy penthouse apartment with my very own landing deck and a retractable ceiling for starbathing oh

22

dear I've just thought two hundred and fifty-seven years is a long time when I do get back they'll have rented that penthouse to someone else and they'll be trying on all my clothes!!!

Julian picked up a flat stone and gloomily sent it skimming across the lake. The whole thing was his fault. If he hadn't prised the spacecraft apart and broken the launching fuel link, Addie wouldn't be in this mess! The stone skipped in three expert arcs across the water. Addie had gone very quiet, and he glanced down at her uneasily, thinking she might be pining from homesickness and it would all be his fault. Maybe she might even die from it!

But Addie didn't look at though she were pining about anything. She was watching the course of the stone with interest, then she licked her finger thoughtfully and held it up to test the wind.

We need an angle of forty-five degrees and if you could aim south of the sun we just might make it . . .

'Make what?' Julian asked, bewildered, trying to decipher the screen script which had become so rapid that the words ran into one another. The screen bounced impatiently up and down in his hand and he almost imagined that he received a small electric shock.

Brother do you need chouls don't be so dense who's worried about RMBZ33 you could eas-ily throw the old bus up with me in it!

Julian shook his head furiously. 'What a crazy idea! Supposing I don't get that hubcap thing up high enough? I'd have to stand here and watch you crash!'

There you go again being negative I never knew such a wimpy negative giant of course you can throw me up high enough no worries and once I catch the edge of the orbital blink it'll be watch my dust pal.

Julian went cold with dismay. It was one thing to flick a newspaper casually on to someone's porch, or send a flat stone skipping across the surface of a lake. He looked at the spacecraft. It wouldn't just be an object he was throwing. Addie would be inside! What if he miscalculated and it went down someone's chimney, or plunged into the lake . . .

Addie calmly put on her helmet and slicked her hair up under it, tucked her pants into the tops of her boots and pulled on her little silver gloves. She climbed into the spacecraft and looked out at him through the porthole, then saluted. The porthole snapped shut and there was no sign in the smooth metal fabric to show that there had ever been a little window there.

Julian slowly picked up the spacecraft which now looked quite ordinary, like a hubcap. That was the best way to think of it, as an old lost hubcap, something to practise discus throwing with. He held it cupped in the palm of his hand and faced the sun. An angle of forty-five degrees . . . and if he made a mistake, Addie would crash into the lake, or over the fence on to the freeway . . . He lowered his arm abruptly. The little metal screen in his other hand seared his palm angrily and he brought it up close to his eyes and read:

What's the delay we've only got ten seconds you big galoot get cracking or I'll come out there and bite you if you're ever up on Polaris

25

13 don't forget to look me up only right now don't let me down love from Addie signing of P.S. I'm glad I met you let's get this show on the airways you and me together. P.P.S. You aren't so dumb for a giant even if you do need chouls!

Julian braced himself and flung the spacecraft forward and up as powerfully as he could. It curved upwards and hung poised above a tree crest and seemed to be pinned, motionless, to the crisp morning air. Agonized seconds passed while he watched, expecting it to crash. He thought he heard a distant faint sound, a humming, like bees reeling through golden clover, and then the spacecraft whizzed up into the sky and disappeared.

'I saw you!' a voice screeched shrilly from behind the lake fence. 'I saw you chucking stones and I'm going to tell Mum! She sent me to find out why you're taking so long over your paper round. I'll tell her, all right, and are you going to cop it! And you'd better give me back that crummy Barbie doll, too. I know it was you who took it!'

Julian turned slowly, his mind still full of his last sight of Addie, resplendent and brave in her silver uniform with all her decorations. Addie saluting him, a space commander top grade supreme saluting HIM! He dragged his mind unwillingly from that glowing memory and looked at Wendy . . . looked at a little dumpy girl with a pouting face, babbling inanities at him. A twitty little face, not worth being bothered about.

He'd go down and watch Luke train for soccer and try out for the team himself, that's what he'd do, that's how he'd spend the rest of Saturday. He set off around the lake, away from Wendy, whistling, striding along on his giant's legs.

'It wasn't a stone,' he called back crushingly over his shoulder. 'You need chouls, you little squirt!'

The Two Chefs

TWO

Mr Napolean's restaurant, Le Café Grand, was famous, and rightly so, for Gustav ruled the kitchen. Gustav's cooking was so brilliant that customers sometimes waited for days to get a booking.

Mr Napolean decided to expand his restaurant.

'I want an assistant chef, then,' said Gustav. He didn't ask politely if he could have one, because he knew very well that the restaurant was prosperous because of him.

Mr Napolean was going to point out that Gustav already had two kitchen assistants, one trainee pastrycook, a boy who did nothing but cut up ingredients for salads, and an expensive dishwasher the size of a spa pool, but he was so much in awe of Gustav that he advertised at once for an assistant chef.

Igor applied, and Mr Napolean sent him out to the kitchen.

Gustav looked at Igor, and Igor looked right back. Most people meeting Gustav for the first time tended to shuffle, look down at the floor and stammer. He had a magnificent moustache like the handlebars of a BMW motorbike and eyes that flashed like police car lights. His chef's cap and apron were hand-laundered daily by a very exclusive laundry. The two kitchen assistants, the trainee pastrycook, the boy who did the salad vegetables, and even Mr Napolean, spoke to him with great respect. But Igor didn't look impressed at all.

Gustav was annoyed and he began to show off. He was making puff pastry at a special marble table he'd bullied Mr Napolean into buying. He handled the pastry as delicately as a violinist tuning a Stradivarius and when he finished, everyone clapped.

Except Igor. He put on his own cap and apron, and Gustav's moustache quivered slightly. Igor's cap was ten centimetres taller than his own, and his apron starchier. It even had his name, Igor, embroidered on the pocket. Then Igor unpacked a carton he'd brought with him, filled with beautiful copper pans and skillets.

'This kitchen is already fully equipped,' said Gustav icily.

'I prefer not to use inferior equipment,' said Igor. He pushed Gustav's pastry aside and began to make a marvellous Hazelnut Mousse.

'You may not use my personal marble-topped table,' Gustav said.

'I don't intend to, after today,' said Igor. 'Mr Napolean must have a porcelain one built specially for me. Marble is very old-fashioned as a working surface. No wonder your puff pastry turned out like a lump of compressed cattle fodder.'

The assistants trembled, waiting for Gustav to erupt into one of his rages that could blister all the enamel from the cooking range. But Gustav, though he turned as purple as an eggplant, didn't say anything. With great dignity, he wrote down that evening's dinner menu on the kitchen blackboard:

Cream Avocado Soup.
Asparagus and Smoked Salmon Quiche.
Steak au Gustav.
Strawberry Champagne Sorbet.

He began to create the Strawberry Champagne Sorbet, as daintily as a ballerina dancing before royalty. He acted as though Igor weren't in the kitchen at all, but Igor didn't seem to know that he was being snubbed.

Igor picked up the chalk and wrote on the other side of the blackboard:

Caviar Pâté.
Chicken Stuffed with Grapes.
Igor's Brandied Mushroom Salad.
Caramel Pears.

Igor set to work preparing his menu. He opened the refrigerator and inspected the contents. 'Aargh!' he cried in disbelief. 'How am I, a genius, to create masterpieces using such inferior, poor quality ingredients!'

The assistants looked fearfully at Gustav, who did all the buying personally.

Igor said, 'I will go to the market tomorrow to choose my own ingredients. It is always a mistake to leave such an important task to underlings.'

Gustav marched out of the kitchen and confronted Mr Napolean. 'Get rid of that Igor immediately!' he roared.

'I can't do that,' said Mr Napolean. 'There are a hundred people coming for dinner tonight. We have to have two chefs, you said so yourself. Besides, Igor had excellent references from the Ritz Hotel. Le Café Grand will be the finest restaurant in the country, now.'

'It already was when I was in charge of the kitchen!' said Gustav.

'Now it will be doubly fine and famous,' said Mr Napolean, gazing happily at the long list of reservations for weeks ahead.

And from then on, bookings became very heavy indeed, for word spread about the two brilliant chefs at Le Café Grand. People queued to get seats for dinner, as they would for a football final, and left enormous tips, not for the waiters, but for Igor and Gustav.

But Igor and Gustav didn't have time to spend any of their tip money. They were too involved in fierce competition with one another.

Gustav rose very early each morning to go to the market to buy the most tender vegetables, so fresh they were still beaded with morning dew.

Igor sneakily rang up a cousin in the country and had even fresher vegetables delivered by express messenger.

Gustav did a crash course in Russian and taught himself how to make Borsch from a secret recipe that had been in the family of the Tsars for centuries.

Igor ordered a set of mixing spoons with his initials set in rhinestones. Gustav looked at them jealously and had a new cap and apron designed by the top fashion designer in Paris.

The two chefs became so competitive that the kitchen assistants, the trainee pastrycook and the boy who did the salad vegetables all had nervous breakdowns and left. Mr Napolean didn't bother to hire people to replace them, because Gustav and Igor were working around the clock anyway, trying to outcook and outsmart each other.

Then the waiters resigned because they were so huffy about no longer getting tips. Mr Napolean didn't mind about losing the waiters either, because Igor and Gustav leapt at the chance of serving the customers personally and receiving praise at first hand. Gustav would rush out to a table with a plate of his marvellous Scallops en Brochette, and when the customer lavished compliments upon him he'd rush back to the kitchen and triumphantly make a notch on his rolling pin.

Igor would hover at the next table with a platter of Artichoke Hearts in a sauce so velvety it would make you warble like an opera singer. After the compliments he'd return to the kitchen to make a score on HIS rolling pin.

It was satisfactory while they stuck to separate tables, but soon they became so jealous of each other that they started to compete for praise from the same customers.

The diners found it very disconcerting. They would take a forkful of Almond Crumbed Whiting in Tangerine Sauce, and eat it under Gustav's blazing stare. 'Delicious, Gustav,' they'd say hastily. 'Quite miraculous.'

Then a Seafood Grand Marnier would be plonked in front of them, and they'd taste it and say, 'Wonderful, Igor. Quite superb!'

And soon neither Igor nor Gustav were satisfied with personal compliments. They began to resent compliments addressed to the other.

'This Peach Torte is an artistic triumph, Gustav, and quite delectable,' said a nervous diner, anxious to please, and Gustav, who hadn't made it, boxed his ears.

'You fool! Only an aardvark would appreciate such poor cooking!' he raged, and ran to fetch a magnificent Bombe Glacé topped with crystallised violets. 'Eat this instead!' he ordered, shovelling up spoonfuls and cramming them into the customer's mouth.

'Delicious,' choked the customer.

Things became so tense that customers tended to band together instead of coming to dine alone at Le Café Grand. They felt safer, but not very much. It was still unnerving to eat dinner with a fierce chef hovering at each end of the table, watching every mouthful you ate.

The customers agreed fearfully that everything was really delicious; they didn't dare do otherwise. They meekly forced down filleted turkey in plum sauce, rum babas slathered with double whipped cream, cantaloupe stuffed with shrimps, devil's food cake and bouillabaisse, all served in higgledy-piggledy order. Soon, the customers stopped coming altogether. Although the food at Le Café Grand was so superb, it wasn't worth all the nervous strain and indigestion, and eventually there were no more bookings.

Gustav and Igor still went to the market every morning to bully the stallholders into selling them the best things. There weren't very many stallholders left at the market. Most of them had gone to work in supermarkets, because they were so scared of Gustav and Igor roaring and snatching things out of one another's hands.

The two chefs continued to cook multiple

courses of fabulous gourmet meals, even though there were no customers left to eat them. The beautiful meals sat on trays going nowhere, and Gustav and Igor had to eat everything themselves at the end of a long, hard day's cooking. Mr Napolean ordered them to stop cooking, but Gustav and Igor both yelled, 'Get out of MY kitchen!'

Mr Napolean retreated to his reception desk and looked at his account ledgers. And finally he knew that Le Café Grand was no longer a sound business investment.

'I'm selling this restaurant,' he said crossly. 'You're both fired and you've only got yourselves to blame.' He flipped the Open sign on the door to Closed, and went away and found himself a nice peaceful job managing a diet clinic rest home.

Igor and Gustav stood in the kitchen beside the porcelain-topped table and the marble-topped table, crowded with exotic herbs they wouldn't let each other use, and their individual omelette pans which they kept chained with special padlocks. Igor gloomily made a Bombe Alaska to soothe his nerves, and Gustav sadly piped chocolate cream stars around the edge of a Quince Flan, but their hearts weren't in it.

'There,' said Gustav mournfully. 'Both of us out of a job. I hope you're satisfied.'

'It was just as much your fault,' said Igor. 'It's going to be awful looking for new jobs at our age. I really liked the oven here, too.'

'And I was so fond of that rotisserie,' said
Gustav. 'I'll never find another one like it.'

'And the red velvet carpet in the dining room,'
said Igor. 'That was so classy! Even the Ritz Hotel
didn't run to red velvet carpets. Perhaps the new
owner will rip it up and put down plastic tiles
instead. I've got a good mind to buy Le Café
Grand myself, to save it from such a fate.'

He opened the casserole dish which held all his
accumulated tip money, but saw with regret that it
wouldn't be quite enough.

Gustav poured out his unspent tip money from
a crockery stockpot. He looked at Igor and Igor
looked at him.

'If we put our money together ...' they both
said.

They had just enough money between them to buy Le Café Grand. They changed the Closed sign to Open and they also decided to rename the restaurant the Grand Café.

'Now,' said Gustav, grabbing the chalk. 'Tonight's menu.' He wrote on the blackboard:

Coq au Vin.

Smoked Ham with Mango Glazing.

Cointreau Blueberries.

'Nonsense,' said Igor reaching for the chalk:

Cheese Soufflé.

Roast Goose and Chestnuts.

Fondant Baskets with Melon and Chocolates.

They glared at each other across the blackboard. Then they looked round at the rich ingredients overflowing from the fridge and spreading over every centimetre of workspace, the cream, the herbs, the fat tender poultry, the grated handmade double-strength chocolate, the velvety sauces. Suddenly both of them felt rather queasy.

'Igor,' said Gustav, reaching for the Alka Seltzer. 'What say we have a simpler menu for this new restaurant of ours?'

'You mean leave out the herbs from the Coq au Vin?' Igor said doubtfully.

'No, this is what I mean,' said Gustav and picked up the chalk and wrote:

Le Boeuf.

La Purée les frites.

Glacé au Chocolat.

Igor studied it.

'Rubbish!' he said. 'You don't mean that at all. What you mean is roast beef, mashed spuds or french fries, and chocolate ice cream for dessert. I don't know about that chocolate ice cream. I rather fancy baked apple pie myself.'

He made the correction on the blackboard and began to shell the peas, whistling cheerfully to himself. Behind his back, Gustav glared. He secretly rubbed out 'baked apple pie'.

Igor's apple pie, he thought pityingly, just would not be in the same class as his own stewed rhubarb and custard.

How Nellie Patch saved the little town of Sycamore

THREE

Although she was only nine, Nellie Patch could talk louder and longer and faster than anyone else in town. Talking was her favourite thing, and had been the cause of the school closing down. All the teachers had nervous breakdowns because of Nellie's chatter, so everyone was obliged to enrol their children for correspondence lessons instead.

Nellie had no trouble at all waking up in the mornings. She LOVED getting up early, because it meant that the day had more hours to talk in. She would go from bed to bed in her house and shake everyone awake.

'Quentin, listen!' she told her little brother. 'There's something pretty strange about our newspaper delivery boy you know how I always wait out the front to chat to him well this morning he suddenly started jumping up and down on the spot

41

rolling his eyes and he tore the newspaper up in little shreds and threw them at me and he was making funny gibbery noises too then he jumped on his bike and raced off down the street do you think he could have been stung by one of those big stripy wasps Quentin are you listening properly wake up . . .'

But Quentin wouldn't. He reached groggily into his bedside table drawer, grabbed a pair of cottonwool earplugs and stuffed them in his ears. Everyone in Nellie's family kept earplugs in the drawers of their bedside tables.

Nellie couldn't understand why the people of Sycamore crossed over to the other side of the street when they saw her coming, but she decided that they were just shy. So, to put them at their ease she would run after them, and say, 'Why good morning Mrs Jenkins what a pity it's raining only it could be worse it could be sunny with just the sound of rain that would be very creepy if you couldn't actually see it falling only hear it all this rain will certainly make the lawns look nice and green and fresh wouldn't it be a good idea if someone invented roll-up lawns they'd always stay green no matter what and wouldn't need mowing and people would have more time for chatting I do love chatting don't you it's such a nice cheerful thing to do to get back on the subject of roll-up lawns unless you'd like me to think up another topic of conversation you could use them as spare carpets too and maybe keep a pet lamb in the living room or maybe even a buffalo . . .'

But by the time Nellie had got to the bit about buffalos, Mrs Jenkins had run desperately into her garage and locked the door. Nellie stayed another ten minutes nattering through the keyhole, but Mrs Jenkins had climbed right inside her compost maker and burrowed deep down in the mulch to block out the noise.

Everyone in that town went around with socks pulled over ears and tea cosies pulled over the socks and crash helmets over the whole lot. Sometimes Nellie would stop talking for a second or two and wonder vaguely why everyone looked

so strange and was so hard of hearing, but she practised making her voice louder and boomier. And soon all the people had to send away for thicker ski socks and professional car racing helmets. They used up all their holiday money and their savings, and began to look at Nellie in a not very friendly way.

One morning there was a loud knocking on the Patchs' front door, and when Mrs Patch opened it, there stood the mayor and the police constable and the school principal and the bank manager, and behind them, everyone else in town. They all looked fed up.

'We're very sorry, Mrs Patch,' they said briskly, 'but the time has come to do something about Nellie. No one comes to the shopping centre anymore because they're afraid they'll meet Nellie and get talked to and not be able to escape. People are moving out of town and everyone is jittery and nervous. We all had a meeting and decided that the only solution is to make Nellie live in the telephone booth outside the town hall until she's grown up and quieter. We fixed the door so it will only open from the outside.'

'Oh dear,' said Mrs Patch. 'It does seem a shame. She's such a nice little girl, or would be if only she didn't talk so much. I'm going to miss her.'

'You'll still be able to keep in contact by phone,' the mayor said kindly. 'Except we've had a technician alter it so that she can't *make* telephone calls to people, only receive them. And we've fitted the phone box up very nicely with crayons and jigsaw puzzles and a little television set. She won't feel lonesome, there are plenty of windows for her to look out of. Come along, Nellie.'

'What a lot of people!' said Nellie happily, suspecting nothing. 'Is there going to be a picnic then I do love picnics specially when they have egg and spoon races why doesn't my spoon ever stay still in my mouth I wonder and the egg always drops off how peculiar having a picnic on Tuesday it's terrific that everyone in town looks cheerful for a change they all usually look so glum and not a bit friendly why are they all crowded around that telephone box outside the town hall is there going to be an ice cream van coming along can I please go over there and stand in the queue so I won't miss out?'

'By all means,' said the mayor. 'You can be first in the queue as a special treat.'

But before Nellie could enter the furnished telephone box, something quite frightening happened. A large sinister UFO, shaped like a long green coffin, dipped down out of the sky and landed in front of the town hall. It certainly didn't belong to friendly visitors. A harsh voice rasped from a loudspeaker turret, 'It is useless to flee! People are to remain exactly where they are!'

The UFO was piloted by aliens from outer

45

space and they had a wicked plan to capture
everyone on earth, starting with the little town of
Sycamore. They climbed out of their spacecraft
and looked coldly at the terrified people. They
were armed with powerful ray guns which could
freeze whole populations and shrink them down to
the size of peanuts, and some metal carrying boxes
ready to pop all the shrunken peanut-sized people
in.

'Now look here ...' said the mayor, but his
teeth were chattering so much he had to stop.

'I think you green people had better leave this
min ...' said the police constable, but he didn't get
very far, either.

The aliens slowly lifted their ray guns. But
before they could take aim, Nellie, beaming at the
sight of two new faces, rushed forward.

'Why hello!' she cried. 'I never saw you in town
to talk to before what smart green scuba diving
suits did you get them mail order from the city and
snorkels too here let me look what a shame there's
nowhere around here you can go scuba diving you
could come to the picnic instead if you like you
certainly are very tall aren't you both my dad's the
tallest man in town in his socks but even he's not as
tall as you do you want to come home and meet my
dad except he's away a lot he had to go into the city
to visit an ear specialist but you could still call at
my house tomorrow for a nice long chat my
address is Number Four Lambert Crescent the
house with all the soundproofing covers over the

windows so the neighbours won't complain my mum says only they still do but I don't know what for it's nice to see some new faces around Sycamore we haven't had any new people for ages not many new people come here to live and it's kind of funny a lot of people seem to be moving away too now I come to think of it and I don't know why because Sycamore is a nice little town . . .'

'Psinty knowp!' the aliens said threateningly in their own language.

'Oh no that's not my name I don't know anyone here called that my name is Nellie Patch I wonder if Cindy Nope was that lady who worked in the hardware shop only she left I could certainly find out for you how about I take you on a guided tour all over Sycamore after we go to the picnic there's going to be free ice cream the mayor said I could have first taste but it's more polite to let visitors go first so I don't mind if you do oh have you both got headaches you poor things it might be the air here a lot of people seem to get headaches do you feel dizzy or something?'

The two aliens clapped their pointy hands over their long pointy ears and backed away from Nellie, staring at her in horror, but she didn't stop talking. She followed them right up to the door of their spacecraft, waving the ray guns excitedly.

'Are these things really snorkels they don't look much like it are they microphones are you making a TV film like the ad they did about green beans

oh how exciting we never had anything like that in Sycamore before can I be in it can I have a ride in your helicopter whatever it is I wouldn't touch anything I promise I'm always very tidy can I come back with you to your television station and see what the advertisement looks like when it's made I always wanted to see inside a television station I wouldn't mind working in one as an announcer you know it would be a nice chatty sort of job and I know I'd just love it . . .'

The two aliens snatched back their ray guns and pushed her firmly off their stepladder.

'Jy erday! Onnet qay whi'd mumn swagar!' they said, meaning, 'Don't you EVER stop talking, you little earbasher? If everyone on this planet is like you, we're off!'

48

They slammed the door and the spacecraft shot up into the sky at a tremendous speed and didn't stop until it reached its own galaxy.

Nellie looked wistfully up at the empty sky, but the mayor and everyone rushed forward and hugged her gratefully and shook her hand. The mayor took off his mayoral chain and let her wear it, and they all said how brave she was to approach two enemy aliens all by herself and save Sycamore and not even be scared by those terrifying ray guns.

Nellie opened her mouth to tell them that she hadn't realized they were ray guns; she'd thought they were snorkels or microphones, but her tongue had finally had enough!

It just refused to work anymore. Nellie crossed her eyes desperately, but try as she would, she couldn't make her tongue move left or right or up or down.

'There,' said her mother. 'I always warned you something like that might happen one day. I hope it teaches you a lesson, Nellie. We'll get the doctor to put a splint on it and if you want to use it again in the future, you must let it have a good long rest.'

It took weeks for Nellie's tongue to recover from the aliens. Everyone made a big fuss of her for saving the town, and as she couldn't talk, she had to listen. She had spent so many years yakking and chattering and nattering that she hadn't known about listening, and to her amazement she found it a novel and enjoyable thing to do.

Glumly

FOUR

At the entrance to the city of Glumly there was a sign which said:

NO LAUGHING. NO WHISTLING.

NO PARTIES.

NO BIRDS ALLOWED. (ONLY VULTURES.)

IF YOU SMILE, MR GRIM WILL PUT YOU IN PRISON.

The prison was usually empty, because nobody ever felt like smiling, anyhow. There was a special grey screen, like a huge canopy, stretched above the city, which prevented the sun's rays shining through. Mr Grim's favourite colour was grey.

Sometimes the canopy developed a crack, and a small amount of sunshine, or a couple of stars, or a section of rainbow would peep through the slit, but Mr Grim had an emergency squad of officers equipped with tins of solution to repair the holes.

In all the city streets there were signs:

KEEP OFF THE CONCRETE. (NO GRASS ALLOWED.)
THIS IS A SERIOUS CITY. NO JOKES.
IF YOU RUN OR HOP OR LOOK FRIVOLOUS,
MR GRIM WILL PUT YOU IN PRISON.

Mr Grim was obviously powerful. He lived in a knobbly, spiked castle with a flag on a tower. The flag didn't flutter, because that would have been frivolous. It was made from thick metal, and had **YOU ARE NOT ALLOWED UP IN THIS TOWER** written on it.

Mr Grim's cook was trained to serve him meals of lumpy potatoes, cold spaghetti, and horrible puddings full of burnt sultanas. He never had visitors at the castle, but they wouldn't have liked it much, anyhow, because the mattresses on the beds were as hard as tree trunks, and all the bulbs had been removed from the bed lamps. There was no hot water, and the rooms had been specially designed to let in as many draughts as possible.

Nobody was allowed to wear any colour except grey in Glumly, and there was a strict rule that faces had to look miserable. So everybody's mouth drooped down at the corners, and every forehead was laced with lines and furrows. People went about saying to each other, 'Unhappy birthday to you!' and the other person would say, 'What's a birthday?' The children in Glumly were encouraged to cry. Mr Grim liked to hear people sounding sad. The only festival they had in the city was a weekly gathering. The person with the most

52

unhappy face won a prize, and the child who could cry the loudest and longest won a prize, and whoever could tell the most depressing thing that had happened to them during the week won a prize. The prizes were grey handkerchiefs, made of rough scratchy cloth, and they made you cry harder if you wiped away tears with them.

Mrs Sorrow would wail, 'Oh, it's been a terrible day! I couldn't get the clothes dry, and then I lost my new grey umbrella, and the milkman's grey horse kicked me!'

'Pah, that's nothing!' Mrs Misery would scoff. 'I didn't get a wink of sleep all night because the baby is teething, and when I got up, I caught my thumb in the tap and was stuck there for two hours!'

'I saw one of those nasty rainbow things through a crack in the canopy,' Billy Frown said dolefully. 'I felt sick all morning because of it!'

It was considered well-mannered to be sick. People boasted about their migraine headaches and their lumbago, and if you woke up feeling fit, you kept it to yourself, because people would give you funny looks, as though you didn't know how to behave politely.

The only visitors to Glumly were small, creeping things, caterpillars and snails and earthworms. And they would crawl and creep as fast as they could from one side of the city to the other, and at the furthest wall they would mutter, 'Oh, what a

53

terrible place!' and 'I didn't like it there!' and 'It was just like wading through a river of wet cement!' The city of Glumly was an extremely miserable place to live, but the people didn't know anything different, because the gates to the city were kept locked.

Billy Frown had a sister whose name was Sarah. Although her family endeavoured to teach her how to look miserable, her mouth tilted up at the corners and her eyes sparkled. She had little dimples which Mrs Frown tried to disguise with grey sticking plaster. And furthermore, Sarah could never master the habit of slouching along with her shoulders hunched, which was the way Mr Grim had ordered the people of Glumly to walk. Sarah's feet looked as though they would skitter into a wild dance, or a shameful hop and skip.

'She's a disgrace to the family!' Mrs Frown lamented. 'There's our Billy, who can look nearly as gloomy as Mr Grim when he tries, and our Laura, head of the Pick-Out-Every-Blade-of-Grass Committee, and me, the lead singer in the Mournful Choir! Sarah, you're just not concentrating. What if Mr Grim sees you with your mouth turned up in that ridiculous way?'

'I can't help it,' said Sarah. 'I keep thinking of things that make it go up like that.'

'What do you mean, child?'

But Sarah didn't want to say, because she knew

54

she would get into trouble. Yesterday she found a small green caterpillar. You were supposed to summon a guard and have snails and caterpillars arrested for trespassing, but she picked it up, making sure nobody saw her. She had thought the caterpillar delightful, with its multiple, busy little legs, and her dimples had popped through the sticking plaster, and her mouth had twitched up at the corners.

When she put the caterpillar back on the concrete, it had twinkled away and under a crack in the city wall as fast as it could go. Sarah had looked under the crack and seen grass blades and a daisy growing on the other side of the wall. She knew it was a flower, because Mr Grim had picture posters in the schoolhouse which said:

THIS IS A PICTURE OF A FLOWER.
IT IS AN UGLY, NASTY, UNNECESSARY, SMELLY THING
AND IT CAN CAUSE A SERIOUS DISEASE
CALLED HAY FEVER.

But the sight of the real flower had made her mouth turn up to her ears.

The Frown family found her a terrible embarrassment. On festival days, when it was her turn to get up on the stage, Sarah could never think of anything miserable to tell. 'Go on, Sarah,' her mother would say encouragingly.

'Um . . .' said Sarah. 'Well now . . . I slept all night. I didn't wake up once.'

'Surely you had a nightmare, little girl?' Mr

55

Grim demanded sternly. But Sarah had dreamed of flying, high above the canopy, on a horse with golden wings. She knew what golden was, because sometimes she had managed to catch a quick glimpse of golden light through the accidental rents in the screen, before they were repaired.

'I didn't like the breakfast porridge, Mr Grim,' she said politely.

'That's nothing,' Mrs Scowler said tartly. 'Nobody likes the breakfast porridge. It's always pre-packaged full of lumps and bits of grit. Can't you do better than that? Didn't you at lease graze your knee today?'

Sarah looked secretive. She had fallen over; she was always falling over, because she kept forgetting that running was forbidden in Glumly. But she had landed on an old wire mattress base, and bounced. (The mattress base was decorating the city square, because Mr Grim liked the look of old junk lying around.) It had felt so marvellous that she had gone on bouncing for five minutes. And bouncing was forbidden in Glumly.

'Mr Grim, sir,' she asked boldly. 'Would you please tell me why bouncing is forbidden?'

Mr Grim drew himself up and looked strict and terrible, because nobody ever dared question his rules. 'Oh my!' everyone whispered. 'That little Frown child will end up in prison!'

Sarah's mother cried anxiously, 'Oh, please don't take any notice of Sarah, Mr Grim! She has a

56

dreadful temperature, and she really doesn't know what she's saying! I'm sure she must be coming down with something painful and serious and dangerous.'

'Take her to the hospital, then,' Mr Grim said, mollified.

Sarah didn't particularly want to go. The hospital was as sad and dreary as an old empty purse, and the nurses wore grey uniforms and the beds were all chilly. They dressed Sarah in a scratchy grey robe and slid her into one of the uncomfortable beds. There were signs all over the ward:

NO VISITORS.

MEDICINE IS TO TASTE AS NASTY AS POSSIBLE.

NOBODY IS ALLOWED TO CHEER ANYBODY ELSE UP.

NO GET-WELL CARDS: PATIENTS ARE EXPECTED TO GET WORSE.

All the patients looked suitably depressed. They had nothing to do but lie in bed and talk about how ill they were and how ill they had been last year. Mr Grim sometimes came around to inspect the hospital and satisfy himself that they were all having a dreadful time. The patient who had been there the longest and had the most aches and pains would be given a prize. It was a hot-water bottle filled with ice cubes.

'May I have something to read?' Sarah asked one of the nurses.

'Why? Just lying there thinking how ill you are

is occupation enough. We don't have books, anyhow, only a medical dictionary and a street directory of the city of Glumly.'

Sarah chose the street directory. As she studied the map she noticed that there was nothing shown outside the city walls. The border of the paper was just filled in with printed warnings:

GLUMLY CITY. ENTRANCE OR EXIT FORBIDDEN.

THIS AND THAT FORBIDDEN.

EVERYTHING FORBIDDEN.

TRESPASSERS PROSECUTED AND PUT INTO PRISON.

MR GRIM, OWNER.

Sarah thought hard. She had peeped through

that crack in the wall and she'd seen grass and a daisy, and the map didn't show them at all.

When the nurse came with a nasty supper on a grey metal tray, (hot orange juice, frozen unthawed noodles and a bunch of sour grapes), Sarah asked, 'Have you ever been outside the city gates, Nurse Steelheart?' and the nurse fainted.

When she recovered, she made agitated moaning noises and stared at Sarah. 'That poor little child is demented!' she cried. 'She was talking to me about . . . about going outside the city walls! Nobody ever mentions such a thing!'

Mrs Frown was sent for and told to take Sarah home, because she was clearly too ill to remain in hospital. 'I feel all right, really I do,' Sarah told her mother.

'Don't talk in that vulgar manner! Nicely brought up people never feel all right! You're much too ill to go to school, that's certain. You must stay at home. Oh dear, if it's not one thing, it's another! Though maybe being so ill might cure you of all that silly grinning and jumping about!'

Sarah didn't mind missing school, although it was hard to find anything interesting to do in Glumly to fill in the hours. Sometimes she went and looked at Mr Grim's castle, and if he happened to be on the tower, glaring down at her, she scowled back, to please him, so she wouldn't be sent back to the hospital. And sometimes she went to watch the sign-writers. They were always preparing new notices:

NOBODY IS TO HAVE CURLY HAIR.

PEOPLE ARE NOT ALLOWED TO COO AT NEW BABIES IN PRAMS.

'Mr Grim certainly is getting strict,' Sarah said to one of the sign-writers.

NEW BABIES ARE NOT ALLOWED TO GURGLE, he wrote.

'New babies can't read,' Sarah said helpfully.

'Are you making a joke, little girl?' he snapped. 'Surely you know that jokes are forbidden!' Sarah quickly forced her mouth down at the corners and went away. She went to the city wall to see if she could find some more caterpillars. The crack was slightly larger, because a hedgehog in a hurry had burrowed through during the night. Sarah peeped through. She saw the grass, and the daisy, and she could hear something beautiful and unusual.

The only music that was allowed in Glumly was sorrowful music played on a grey organ, which everybody had to go and listen to each afternoon, and you were expected to cry. The organ music was accompanied by the Mournful Choir.

This was music, but quite different. It was sweet and lilting, and not sorrowful at all. It made your feet feel as though they must run and run and weave crazy patterns all over the city square. Sarah slipped her hand through the crack and the music stopped; there was a rustling, and then silence. She had frightened the music away. She thought it might have been a bird. The picture poster in the schoolhouse said:

THIS IS A DRAWING OF A BIRD.
BIRDS ARE NOISY, WAYWARD, FOOLISH CREATURES,
AND DO NOT KNOW HOW TO BE DIGNIFIED CITIZENS.

Sarah began to work on the crack, pulling away chips of mortar and stone, making the crack large enough for both hands to fit through. Then she had to stop, because it was time to go to the afternoon concert in the city square. This was compulsory, to make sure that the people went home to supper each day in a proper state of melancholy. Before the concert started, Mr Grim read out a list of all the things that wouldn't be available tomorrow. No butter, no boot polish, everybody could have three small lumps of coal only for their fires, combs would no longer be produced at the factory. SOME people were combing their hair much too often, and even looking as though they enjoyed it.

'Oh, dear!' said everyone, shocked. 'Oh, my goodness, what an awful thing to do! It certainly wasn't me!'

'Total sad silence for the gloomy organ music!' cried Mr Grim. He had a special platform con- structed, draped in murky material, and he played the organ himself. Just as he sat down to play, and the ladies of the Mournful Choir cleared their throats for the first verse of 'Life Is Always Grey and Weary', a small bird flew through Sarah's crack in the wall. It darted about under the charcoal-coloured canopy which was the sky of Glumly, and it sang. Everybody listened in astonishment, and a baby in a pram laughed.

'Stop that baby laughing, or I shall put it in prison!' said Mr Grim sternly. He sent some of his guards to catch the bird and put IT in prison for trespassing, but the bird simply flew out of reach.

Sarah watched very closely. Usually she didn't even bother to look up at the horrid grey canopy which covered Glumly. It was interesting only when the repair men climbed the scaffolds to fix rips and dents. It was just there, and always had been, an enormous brooding, billowing cloud above their heads.

The little bird pecked briskly at a weak spot in the canopy, a shaft of brilliant sunlight arrowed through, and the bird flew out and away, singing. Mr Grim covered his eyes and yelled, 'Guards! Climb up at once and repair the hole! That golden stuff is evil and poisonous!' Mothers quickly shielded their children's eyes and ran into their houses while the repair work was being carried out.

But that shaft of sunlight had dropped straight down on Sarah's upturned face, and it had felt softly warm, and not evil at all.

That night, when everyone slept, she found a pair of big, sharp scissors and crept out into the city square. She climbed the scaffolding and felt above her head. There was the canopy, chill and rubbery and unpleasant to touch. It reminded her of a dinosaur's skin. The picture poster in the schoolhouse said:

THIS IS A DINOSAUR,
LARGE, GREY AND GLOOMY.
A FINE TYPE OF CITIZEN.
NOW UNFORTUNATELY EXTINCT.

Sarah thought she would make lots of holes, so that the bird could fly back in whenever it pleased, and the sunshine spill through again. She thought that it would be worth being put into Mr Grim's prison just to have that happen. She poked with the scissors and made a hole, then she snipped a long length and ripped it apart with her hands.

She walked along the scaffold and made big holes wherever she could reach. Then she stopped and looked.

There was no sunshine, but something else. Above the canopy, an immense distance away, there were thousands and thousands of tiny twinkling things, like little lamps. They didn't move or fly, but seemed to be dancing up and down in the one spot, and some were very bright, and others faint and far away, but they all danced. Hanging on invisible threads in the air and dancing!

Sarah looked at them for a long time, and when she got down, she gathered all the containers of instant canopy repair solution and hid them down an empty well. Then she went home and waited for morning.

And in the morning people gathered in the city square, dazzled and afraid. The little dancing lights had vanished, but sunlight rippled through the long rips Sarah had made. And other things had come in, too. They were like flowers. Flowers with wings, fluttering about the grey streets of Glumly. And there were other floating things, like puffs of smoke attached to delicate stems, and they drifted and settled on people's startled, upturned faces.

'Collect all those unspeakably gaudy butterflies and those dandelion seeds at once!' ordered Mr Grim. 'This is a state of emergency! Everyone is to climb the scaffolds and repair the canopy!' He marched up to his castle tower to make sure that they obeyed. 'This is the worst calamity the city has ever had!' he said, which should really have given him great satisfaction, but he was too annoyed to enjoy it because the people kept gaping at the butterflies instead of catching them.

'They're too fast for anyone to catch,' said the guards. 'And, we can't find the instant canopy repair solution either, Mr Grim, sir. We've looked everywhere.'

'Open the city gates and chase all those butter-flies out. Then everyone has to get busy and make a new batch of repair solution!'

The city gates hadn't been opened for eighty years. They creaked and grumbled and groaned, and when the guards shoved at them harder, they crumbled away from their old iron hinges and fell in a pile of grey rubble. Sunlight spilled through the gates in a great golden tide.

Sarah looked out. There was a wide green meadow starred with yellow flowers, and more butterflies and birds and water, a silver ribbon of it, dancing through the meadow. Sarah ran outside.

'Sarah Frown, you come back inside this minute!' cried her mother, horrified. 'You'll catch some awful disease out there, it's so bright and colourful! Oh, I wish the guards would fix up the canopy and get Glumly back to normal!'

Sarah climbed up on the city wall and looked over the top of the grey canopy which covered

Glumly. It seemed like a lid on a box, and she wondered what would happen if she took the lid away completely. Mr Grim would most surely put her in prison, but she didn't care. She took hold of a section of the canopy and tugged it loose. Then she walked along the framework ripping away great sections of canopy, and looked down at all the upturned faces of the people in Glumly.

'Stop her!' some of them cried. 'It's that awful little Sarah Frown whose mouth goes up at the corners! The one who's always hopping and whistling!'

Sarah felt like whistling now, and she did, because there was something mad and exciting about tearing away the grey covering from Glumly. The sun splashed down into the little streets and lanes, and Sarah thought that all the houses looked very much prettier.

'Everything looks wonderful with the sun on it!' she called down to the faces. 'Do look!'

'Things aren't supposed to look wonderful!' they reminded her crossly.

'Why not?' asked Sarah.

'Because Mr Grim says so!' But the people glanced thoughtfully at the houses and one of the women murmured, 'Oh dear, my windows could do with a good clean. I never realized how grimy they were. They don't look a bit nice!' and then stopped, realizing uneasily what she had said.

Sarah climbed all over the framework, pulling

away the canopy. Mr Grim scrambled about on his tower, trying to stop her, but she dropped a smothery bundle of canopy on his head. Some of the children wandered through the city gates and outside. Their parents called them back sharply, but the children had discovered that grass was wonderful stuff to roll in, and there were no notices in the meadow saying it was forbidden.

A boy from a neighbouring village, riding by on a horse, stopped and looked at the broken gates, and at Sarah up on the framework, and everyone milling about. He knew that the people of Glumly were quite peculiar, and lived locked up inside a great grey umbrella, but he was a polite boy so he just said mildly, 'Good morning. Are you folks having a picnic? Nice day for it.'

The Glumly people stared. Nobody said, 'Good morning' in Glumly. They said, 'What a horrible day!' or 'More dreary hours to get through!' or 'The breakfast porridge is getting worse and worse!' And they didn't know what a picnic was.

'What's a picnic?' they asked.

'Why, you take your food down by the river, and sing and play games, and have a good time. That's what a picnic is.'

The boy didn't wear a single thing that was grey. He had on a red checked shirt, a yellow straw hat, bright blue pants, and wore little gold rings in his ears.

'Go away at once, or I'll have you put in prison!' Mr Grim ordered, finally struggling out from the pile of torn canopy material. 'How dare you look so bright and cheerful!'

'Who's that old misery up there on the tower?' the boy asked Sarah. 'The one with the face like a pail of sour milk?'

'That's Mr Grim,' Sarah said. 'He owns this city.'

'Rubbish,' said the boy. 'Nobody owns a city. It belongs to everyone.'

People muttered amongst themselves and repeated what he'd said and glanced thoughtfully up at Mr Grim. He jumped up and down on his tower with total rage. 'Get back inside the walls at once!' he thundered. 'Or I'll have you ALL put in prison!'

'It's not big enough to hold everyone,' Sarah

68

said. She snatched away the last piece of canopy, and the sun roared into Glumly, and the people stopped being afraid.

They went out through the gates and removed their shoes and tentatively paddled in the river. Some of them picked daisies and decorated their hair, and a very old lady suddenly remembered how to make a daisy chain. Mouths that had turned down at the corners for years were starting to turn creakily upwards. Mrs Gloom said, 'My corns have stopped hurting!' and Mr Dour said, 'My lumbago is better!' and they smiled at each other. Some bold people ventured into Mr Grim's castle, because nobody was doing any normal work and the whole morning was so very extraordinary. They wandered all over the castle, and in the dungeons they found great boxes of balloons and necklaces and chocolates and brightly coloured hats which had been sent to Glumly by various charitable organizations over the years, but Mr Grim had locked the parcels away.

'Put those presents back immediately!' Mr Grim yelled. 'Presents are frivolous time-wasting objects and I won't allow any citizen of Glumly . . .'

'What's this "allowing" business?' someone who had just tasted chocolate for the first time in his life muttered resentfully.

'Put those necklaces down!' shouted Mr Grim. 'Jewellery is forbidden!'

'"Forbidden" did he say?' said someone else. 'I happen to LIKE these red beads and they're staying around my neck! Forbidding and not allowing and threats . . . I'm tired of it. Aren't you tired of it, Mrs Scowler, dear?'

Mrs Scowler had found a lovely orange apron. She suddenly ripped her grey one off and crumpled it into a ball and tossed it disdainfully in Mr Grim's direction. 'There,' she said. 'You like grey so much, YOU wear it . . . you old misery!'

'Stop that!' cried Mr Grim, outraged. 'How dare you! All you disobedient people are to return to your homes this minute, or . . .'

But nobody took the slightest notice of him. He ran about slapping people's hands away from chocolates and books and balloons, but they just swatted him away as though he were a troublesome fly, and his voice dwindled away to a squeak and then to silence.

Nobody knew what to do with the balloons, but the boy on the horse showed them. He was a very patient boy. He answered all their difficult questions, such as, 'But what's a necklace for?' and 'What do we do with the silver paper round these chocolates?' and 'What do you mean, two-legged race?'

Sarah came down from the scaffolding, because she felt it was safe enough now. Mr Grim's guards were lying in the grass by the river, eating chocolate and wearing party hats. And besides, Mr

70

Grim was leaving. He had packed his suitcase and was wheeling it away on top of the sorrowful grey organ, declaring that he wasn't going to live amongst such a crowd of idle, chattering, smiling people.

But nobody had time to say goodbye to him. The people of Glumly were already breaking down the city walls and the scaffolding. It seemed foolish to leave them there, now that the gates were down and the grey canopy gone.

And besides, they had a much lovelier canopy now. It was clear and beautiful and blue, and didn't need any scaffolding at all.

Zarab-Hasaka

FIVE

Zarab-Hasaka had been sealed inside the little green bottle for several hundred years. He couldn't see out because it was made of carved jade, and he spent the centuries feeling sorry for himself. You'd have thought that when someone found the bottle cast up by the sea, he would have been grateful. But he was so tetchy with boredom that when Joanna Mullen took the bottle to her house and removed the stopper, he burst out in a fiery cloud of emerald smoke and scolded her in ancient Arabic for ten minutes.

'WOW!' said Joanna, her eyes as big as puddings. 'A real live genie!'

Zarab-Hasaka, dressed in billowing green satin trousers and a turban decorated with rather flashy emeralds, was most impressive to look at. He had long green fingernails and snappy black eyes, and

73

was so tall that his turban bumped against the ceiling of her room. Joanna was glad when he sat down, cross-legged, on a beanbag chair. 'I am Zarab-Hasaka, the genie of the green flask,' he said grumpily. 'Your wish is my command.'

He wasn't really very enthusiastic about granting any wishes that Joanna might dream up. He didn't think much of her, to tell the truth. In the first place, she had short yellow hair, and all the young ladies he knew had lustrous midnight hair falling to the heels of their little gold pointy-toed slippers. Joanna wasn't even wearing golden slippers, just plastic beach thongs. Zarab-Hasaka thought her clothes were pretty weird altogether. She wore a tee shirt with a picture of a worm coming out of an apple, and not one single jewel, only a bar of silver on her teeth.

Zarab-Hasaka looked around her room. He had no experience of houses, and thought it was a tent, since it clearly wasn't a palace. It was a terrible tent in his opinion, fashioned from hard stiff material, and not very big. There wasn't one Persian carpet anywhere, and Zarab-Hasaka thought it was well beneath his dignity to have his flask opened by such a lowly person.

Joanna's first instinct was to rush out and tell her mum and dad that she'd found a genie in an old green bottle washed up on Hopkin's Beach, but she stopped and considered. It would be more of a surprise, she thought, to keep Zarab-Hasaka a

74

secret, and make her family become suddenly as rich as sultans without telling them how. She thought, however, that she'd have the first wish all to herself.

'I'd like a really terrific album collection, please,' she said. 'I wish one whole wall of my room was filled up with albums.'

'Albums?'

'You know, records . . .'

The genie, rather insulted at being given such a pathetic little wish for his first assignment, twitched his green eyebrows, and in a blink, Joanna's bedroom wall was filled from the ceiling to the floor with large stone slabs. Joanna lifted one with difficulty and looked at it. It was covered with hieroglyphic pictures of people leading oxen and carrying dead ducks and making pottery. She thought it would be bad mannered to show the genie that she was disappointed.

'There are two little words called "thank thee".' Zarab-Hasaka said sternly. 'You should be grateful. Those records are best quality stone engraved by the chief scribe of the Caliph of Ozella.'

'Thank thee. Those records are just great,' Joanna lied. 'I'll be careful not to scratch them.'

'Have you no further wishes?' demanded Zarab-Hasaka, knowing from past experience that new genie owners tended to go a bit overboard in the first few hours of opening the jade bottle. It was best to let them cram their tents with greedy possessions until the novelty wore off.

'I'd like a really nice present for my mum,' said Joanna. 'It's her birthday today, and all I've been able to buy her is a maidenhair fern going brown at the edges because it was on special at the supermarket. Now, let's see, what would she like?'

'A bushel of pearls?' suggested the genie, in a bored voice, rattling off his birthday gift suggestion list. 'Lapis lazuli toe rings, a solid gold anklet adorned with a ruby as big as a roc's egg, or a set of very expensive perfumes and unguents imported from the Nile?'

'What she'd really like is some help in the kitchen,' Joanna said.

'A dishwasher,' she added, but Zarab-Hasaka had already flicked his eyebrows. Joanna heard a yelp from the kitchen, and shot out there.

Mrs Mullen was staring with surprise at a huge, toffee-coloured slave, the size of a campervan. He wore gold hooped earrings and a big scimitar in his sash. He'd shoved Mrs Mullen away from the table and was setting out his own personal collection of cooking utensils, all of them rather ancient and odd looking. He seemed to have taken over the total management of the kitchen.

'He just turned up,' Mrs Mullen whispered to Joanna, bewildered. 'One minute there I was listening to talkback on the radio, and the next thing there HE was, clattering down all those flagons and things and snatching the pastry bowl

76

out of my hands. I know I agreed at the High School Ladies' Auxiliary Committee meeting that I'd let students come here and do work experience in cooking, but I never thought they'd send along a creepy-looking kid like that. He looks too old to be in Year 9, anyhow. And he didn't even bring along an apron.'

The slave, whose name was Careb, tipped a whole packet of dates into the scone mixture, followed by a pot of honey.

'They're supposed to be cheese scones,' Mrs Mullen pointed out, but Careb didn't like to be advised about cooking, and hissed like a boa constrictor at Mrs Mullen through his big white teeth. 'I'll just see to the laundry,' she said nervously.

Joanna went back to Zarab-Hasaka.

'About the dishwasher in the kitchen,' she began.

'Is not the slave Careb to your liking?' Zarab-Hasaka demanded, sounding so affronted that Joanna said quickly, 'Oh yes, he's lovely. Could I have a present for my father, too?'

Zarab-Hasaka thought privately that Joanna's father didn't deserve a present, if he allowed his daughter to run around without wearing a face veil, and no kohl eyeliner, and not one jewel except a skinny band of silver across her teeth.

'Dad won't want any records or a slave like Careb,' Joanna said. 'What he'd really like is his very own video.' Zarab-Hasaka looked blank. 'He likes watching variety shows on TV,' Joanna explained. 'And musical comedy films, that sort of thing. You know, dancing and singing ...'

'Oh, that,' said Zarab-Hasaka squashingly, and flickered his eyebrows. 'Why didn't you say so in the first place?'

Joanna went into the living room where her dad had gone to read the newspaper Motor Supplement. But he wasn't there by himself. He was surrounded by three beautiful young ladies. One of them was fanning him with a palm branch, one was feeding him chubby velvet grapes off a silver tray, and the other one was dancing and singing. They all wore gauzy trousers caught in at the

ankles, and tops made from hundreds of little coloured sequins. They had lustrous dark hair and eyes, and glittered with jewels; they even had a diamond each in their navels. Joanna's dad was looking quite surprised and had put aside his newspaper.

'Kevin!' said Mrs Mullen, who had just come in from the laundry.

'I don't know how they got in here,' Mr Mullen said hastily. 'I didn't invite them. I don't even know them.'

Mrs Mullen clearly didn't believe him. 'I wouldn't mind if they were nice ladylike girls, but the way they're dressed, and in front of Joanna too!' she said crossly. Joanna was thinking how smart the girls looked, and was wondering if she could persuade her mum to let her buy an outfit the same — gauzy pants and a brief little top made of gold threads and sequins — but she could tell by Mrs Mullen's face that she wouldn't be allowed.

Mr Mullen tried to get up from his chair, but the girls wouldn't let him. One of them was rubbing perfumed lotion into his bald spot, and one was sitting on his knee. 'If you knew how silly you looked, Kevin!' Mrs Mullen said, annoyed, and marched outside to hang out the washing.

Joanna went back to Zarab-Hasaka. 'That wasn't what I meant at all,' she said. 'Can't you change it?'

'Change it? I'll have you know those girls are

the best dancers from the household of the Grand Vizier himself. Their names are Zadah, Alzena, and Zenobia. And it wasn't easy getting them here, I can tell you.'

'You'd better send them back,' said Joanna. 'I don't think my mother likes them.'

'Once the shadow is cast by Zarab-Hasaka, genie of the green flask, it rests forever upon the rock,' said the genie smugly.

Joanna sighed. Owning a genie was proving to be more complicated that she thought possible. 'I don't think mum will let him keep those dancing girls in the house,' she said 'but maybe she'll let him keep them out in the garage. Perhaps I'd better get a joint present for both of them, to smooth things over. Something for the holidays. You can't think how cramped it is staying at Grandma's flat in Perth. I think they'd like a nice big caravan. Can you fix it?'

The genie shot her a pained green look and twitched his eyebrows.

Joanna rushed away to look at the new caravan, but couldn't open the back door. Something was leaning against it, something quite large, so she climbed out through the laundry window and found out why the back door was hard to open.

The yard was full of camels, hitched up together, tail to nose, and they were laden with vats of oil, wineskins and other household goods, and what looked like a collapsible tent. Mrs

Mullen, squeaking with indignation, was trying to shoo them away from her clean washing. The whole yard smelled strongly of camel, and there were large spreading footprints patterning the vegetable bed. There were two men in charge of the camels, but they were squatting on the patio playing dice, and couldn't speak English.

'I don't know how your Uncle Barry and Aunt Winifred are going to park their car in the drive tonight when they come for dinner,' said Mrs Mullen. 'I don't know what they're going to think. It was bad enough your father inviting all those hussies home, and now this!'

'Perhaps the camels are being taken to a circus and they just stopped in here to have a rest,' Joanna said guiltily. 'I'll go and telephone and find out.' But instead she climbed back into her room.

'Thanks very much for the camel train and the tent, Zarab-Hasaka,' she said 'but the Council mightn't let us keep them here permanently. Could you please send them back to where you got them?'

'Once the shadow is cast, the rock is forever engraved,' the genie said, glaring at her with his fierce black eyes. 'I am weary of telling you! Are you not pleased with the magnificent camels gracing this miserable oasis?' He looked so strict and terrible that Joanna nodded hastily, and he added, appeased, 'Your wish is my command. What is your bidding?'

'Maybe I'll try a simpler wish,' said Joanna. 'I haven't got anything for my two sisters yet. They're at tennis, but it would be nice to have a surprise present for them when they get back. Angela always wanted some pet lizards, and Cheryl likes cats.'

'Do you choose to waste my powers on so trivial a matter?' Zarab-Hasaka said disdainfully, but flicked his eyebrows, and Joanna went around the house searching for the new pets.

The lizards were in the bathroom. Two of them. There wasn't enough space for any more than that, because crocodiles take up a great deal of room. Joanna hurriedly slammed the door shut on their long clicking jaws and yelled, 'MUM!'

Mrs Mullen came and peeped cautiously around the door at the two large crocodiles slithering in and out of her beautiful blush-pink bathtub.

'Who put those creatures in there?' she demanded. 'It's obvious no one can use that room unless they wear cricket pads on their shins. Aunt Winifred and Uncle Barry will have to use the en suite if they want to wash their hands.'

But Aunt Winifred, when she arrived, didn't even want to go into the front bedroom, because the new cat was stretched out on the bed there, kneading its claws in and out of the quilt. 'I've been told leopards have very nasty temperaments,' she said. 'It seems a peculiar sort of pet to get for

82

the girls, Dorothy. Expensive to feed, too, I dare say. And how much did that sapphire collar round its neck cost? I thought you said you were too broke to come to my Tupperware party this week?' She shot Mrs Mullen a very snaky look, and aimed another one at the dinner arrangements. Careb the slave had arranged cushions on the floor and cut off the legs of the dining room table. There were platters of stuffed olives and figs, fluted silver goblets filled with wine, saffron-flavoured rice and spiced mutton, and a great heap of pomegranates.

'I like a nice plain roast with baked pumpkin and Yorkshire pudding myself,' said Aunt Winifred disparagingly.

Careb stood at the head of the table with his massive arms folded and looked so touchily proud of his cooking skills that no one dared leave the tiniest bit on their plates. As soon as they finished one helping, he gave them new servings of something else, and if they tried to refuse, he whipped out his scimitar and whistled it around their ears threateningly. While dinner was going on, the dancing girls put on a floor show.

'Who are those girls?' Aunt Winifred demanded.

'Friends of Kevin,' Mrs Mullen said stiffly.

'Zadah, Alzena and Zenobia,' said Joanna. 'They're belly dancers.'

It was plain that Aunt Winifred didn't think they were suitable to have at a family dinner, but the girls didn't take any notice of her. In between dancing they fussed around Mr Mullen, offering him the best olives, fanning him with the palm branch and peeling pomegranates for him.

Mrs Mullen had planned to serve coffee out on the patio, but couldn't because of the camel drivers. Their dice game was growing noisy, and it was apparent that they couldn't agree about the rules. They kept snatching sharp little daggers out of their belts and yelling at one another, but when that happened, Careb thrust a powerful arm through the window and yanked them up by their turbans, with their heels dangling in the air. He was so big and scary looking that the camel drivers would put their daggers meekly away.

Joanna could tell by her mother's expression that she was very embarrassed because dinner was turning out this way. She slipped secretly away to her own room. 'Your wish is my command,' said Zarab-Hasaka irritably as soon as she put her head around the door.

'I don't want any more presents,' Joanna said. 'They always end up being a bother. I'd like you to get back inside that bottle, please, so I can throw you back into the sea for someone else to find. Aunt Winifred isn't speaking to Mum because the leopard laddered her pantyhose, and Mum isn't speaking to Dad because she thinks he met all those girls at the Motor Show and invited them here, and Dad's mad because of the camels all over his vegetable garden, and the camel drivers are getting sick of playing dice and want to go on to the next oasis, and Careb the slave can't get any crosser because he's so nasty to begin with.'

'When the shadow is cast ...' began Zarab-Hasaka pompously, looking down his nose at her.

'I know all about that. Please, won't you get back into that bottle?'

'For hundreds of years I had nothing to look at except green jade,' said the genie. 'So boring. There is no way you can get me back in there, I'm telling thee! I am here for good.'

'Oh, it's just too bad! I don't know what you had to give me all those terrible presents for!' Joanna cried, stamping her foot. 'I just wish now I'd asked for an ordinary old magic carpet!'

She heard the echo of a shriek from the living room and ran out there. The room was empty, and she stuck her head out of the window. Hovering some distance above the house roof was their wall-to-wall carpet. Luckily, the carpet wasn't heading off in any direction. It remained stationary, but it was clear that none of its passengers was enjoying the experience, except maybe the dancing girls. A date came plummeting down, followed by a sesame seed bun. 'Don't make it dip down your side, Winifred,' she heard her mum say. 'You'll have us all tipped off onto the roof.'

'I told you not to buy your carpet from Clegg's,' Aunt Winifred said crossly. 'Everyone knows they sell poor quality stuff.'

'Joanna, fetch a ladder,' her dad called down, and Joanna pushed a way through the camels into the toolshed, but the ladder wasn't nearly long enough. She had to telephone the fire brigade, and they had to bring out a snorkel truck all the way from the main city station. The fire chief wasn't pleased about it at all, specially as there was no fire. He got everyone down from the carpet, giving them some very odd looks, but the carpet itself refused to be rescued. Every time he made a grab at it, it bobbed skittishly out of reach, so he had to leave it up there in the sky.

'I could do with a nice cup of tea after all that,' Mr Mullen said when the fire truck left.

But Careb only made some coffee so thick and

strong that it was like trying to drink mocha-flavoured concrete. 'Can't we even get a decent cup of tea around this house anymore?' Mr Mullen growled. He was so seasick after being whisked up into the sky on the living room carpet that even the dancing girls with their pretty black eyes didn't distract him. He just looked at them glumly and rather wished they'd go away so he could watch the seven o'clock news in peace.

Aunt Winifred and Uncle Barry went huffily back to their own place, swearing that they wouldn't ever come back to visit till the Mullens had got rid of all those smelly camels in the yard, the bossy young man in the kitchen, the quarrelsome camel drivers, the crocodiles and the leopard. Not to mention the dancing girls, though it was Aunt Winifred who made more fuss about them than Uncle Barry did.

Joanna marched into her room and looked sternly at the genie.

'To hear is to obey,' Zarab-Hasaka said, yawning.

'You get back inside that little green bottle this instant!'

'No,' he said. 'I won't, and you can't make me, either.'

Joanna had no idea of how to set about cramming a large, imposing genie into a flask the size of a glue bottle against his will, and when she made a tentative snatch, he started to smoke and crackle alarmingly in a shower of green sparks. Joanna stepped back quickly.

'Wouldn't you like a nice little sea cruise?' she coaxed.

'Not in a green jade flask,' said Zarab-Hasaka stubbornly.

In desperation, Joanna ran around the house looking for appealing, attractive bottles. She fended off the crocodiles in the bathroom with the polishing mop, and grabbed up some perfume bottles. There were three, all very beautiful, with elegant scrolled labels and gold stoppers. She took them in to show the genie. 'Anyone would be proud to have a smart little house like this one,' she wheedled, showing him the Chanel Number Five, which her mum had won at Bingo, but the genie just turned up his nose at all of them.

Joanna fetched the crystal wine decanter from the living room, but Zarab-Hasaka wasn't impressed.

She braved the leopard in the front bedroom, and Careb in the kitchen, and staggered back to her room with every bottle she could carry: hand lotion, bath crystals, shampoo and after-shave bottles; vanilla essence and peppermint essence, imported Scottish marmalade and cooking sherry bottles, and laid them out like an enticing shop window display on the floor of her room. Zarab-Hasaka looked them over patronisingly, and rejected every single one.

Joanna was about to burst into tears of mingled frustration and rage, when he picked up a half-empty bottle that had got in amongst the others by accident, and took off its lid.

It was an eight-sided tomato ketchup bottle, and Zarab-Hasaka turned it around and around thoughtfully. 'Eight windows!' he said. 'And a different view from each one, magnificent! And such a fragrance! I wouldn't mind at all, being the genie of such a wondrous flask!' And without saying one more word, he flicked his eyebrows and popped into the tomato ketchup bottle in a little farewell puff of emerald smoke, laced with spurts of tomato ketchup.

Joanna twisted the cap on tightly and held the bottle up to the light, but there was nothing to be seen. Then she took it down to Hopkin's Beach and threw it out onto the tide. 'Goodbye, Mr Zarab-Hasaka,' she said respectfully, but she wasn't really very sorry to see the last of that genie. She rode her bike home, whistling.

'I don't think we'll have any more peculiar things happening at our house,' she said to her mother. 'I think it's all over.'

'It's not,' said her mother crossly. 'We have to get rid of a leopard with a sapphire collar, two crocodiles, three dancing girls, a work experience student with a bad temper and a scimitar, two bickering camel drivers and a whole string of camels, plus a carpet floating above our house and interfering with the television reception. Not to mention all those stone tablet things in your room.'

Joanna rang up the zoo and they came and took away the crocodiles and the leopard. She showed Careb a very good job for a live-in housekeeper-cook advertised in the paper. It offered an enormous salary, and Careb hurried off to terrorize all the other applicants with his scimitar so he could get the job. Then Joanna helped her mother put all the dancing girls in the car, and they drove them to an Arabian café which had a nightly floor show. The manager liked their dancing so much he hired them straightaway.

The carpet was difficult, but they finally managed to get it down by shooting holes in it with some plastic tubing and dried lentils. Back in the living room, it kept billowing up to the ceiling or trying to get out of the window, but they managed to anchor it to the floor with encyclopedia volumes.

They found a circus willing to take the camels and the two camel drivers, but they had to throw in the new tent as a bribe. It was a gorgeous tent.

Joanna went to see it when it was erected on the circus site. It was made of scarlet and purple striped silk, and lined with midnight-blue damask patterned with embroidered gold stars and planets. The circus changed its name from 'Adleys – The Greatest Show On Earth' to 'Adleys – The Greatest Show In The Universe'.

The stone records weren't a problem, as Mr Mullen found they were just the thing to pave the area around the barbecue.

'There,' said Joanna to her mother with relief. 'Now it's finished.'

'Thank goodness for that,' said Mrs Mullen. 'That young man forgot to take his cooking utensils with him, he was in such a hurry to rush off to apply for that job. Clear them away, Joanna, while I get on with making my cheese scones.'

Careb had left behind some earthenware pots and a goatskin pourer and a little fondue cooking lamp.

'It looks very old and dirty,' said Mrs Mullen. 'I wouldn't fancy eating fondue cooked over that.'

'It would make a nice little candlestick for when we have electricity blackouts,' said Joanna. She picked up a sponge and rubbed some of the grime away so she could see the metal underneath.

There was a great burst of orange and an enormous, powerful-looking genie popped out of the spout.

'I am Ahmed-Hassam, genie of the lamp,' he boomed in a loud voice. 'Thy wish is my command.'

ABOUT THE AUTHOR

Born in Kempsey, New South Wales, Robin Klein is one of nine children. Her great-grandfather was an Irish convict who was sentenced to life transportation to Australia for highway robbery.

She had her first short story published at the age of sixteen, and won her only school prize for writing. In 1981 she was awarded a Literature Board grant for writing and since then she has had more than twenty books published. Many have been shortlisted for the Australian Children's Book of the Year Award, including *People Might Hear You* (1984), *Hating Alison Ashley* (1985) and *Halfway Across the Galaxy and Turn Left* (1986) (all available in Viking Kestrel and Puffin). In 1984 *Penny Pollard's Diary* was highly commended and *Thing* was the Australian Junior Book of the Year in 1983.

Now a full-time writer, Robin Klein lives in a bluestone house in the hills near Melbourne with one of her four children.

ALSO BY ROBIN KLEIN

Hating Alison Ashley

Life was difficult at Barringa East Primary where the
teachers tended to have nervous problems and everyone
called you 'Yuk'.

However, Erica Yurken knew she was destined for a
glittering career on the stage. She had never had any doubts
about her own genius. She felt superior to everyone in
Barringa East, even the School Principal and the visiting
District Inspector.

That is, until Alison Ashley started at Barringa East
Primary . . .

Alison Ashley excelled at everything. She was beautiful,
rich, clever and as well-behaved as a nativity angel. She also
lived outside Barringa East - on exclusive Hedge End Road.

But Erica was determined to show up Alison Ashley - and
the annual school camp would be the ideal place!

Hating Alison Ashley – The Play

Adapted for the stage by Richard Tulloch.

Robin Klein's award-winning novel is now a successful
stage play.

CAST:	Minimum 7 (5 female and 2 male) to play 14 roles, but, depending on the numbers available, other characters could be added for crowd scenes.
DURATION:	Two acts of 50-55 minutes each.
AGE SUITABILITY:	10 years and upwards.

Have fun putting on your own classroom production
of *Hating Alison Ashley.*

'I don't think I can bear this exile,' said Mother on the family's second day on planet earth.

'It may not be for as long as we think,' replied X. 'At any moment Lox could beam us saying, "Come home, all is forgiven".'

But it wasn't to be as easy as that. Even with their extraterrestrial powers, learning earth customs caused all sorts of problems for the crazy alien family from Zyrgon . . .

Frances, who had spent her life moving from one rented flat to another, was excited about going to a proper house to live. Her aunt's recent marriage to Mr Tyrell meant that she would have three new cousins, one the same age as herself.

But things were not as she expected. On her first morning in the large, gloomy house, she was introduced to the 'rules'. 'You are not to raise your voice or make a noise,' they told her. 'People might hear you.'

The rules also meant that nobody could enter or leave the house at will. None of the Tyrell girls had ever attended school; the rules forbade it. Their daily life was strict, regimented and supervised.

At first, Frances trustingly accepted her aunt's commitment to Mr Tyrell, and to the mysterious 'temple', with its strange, fanatical beliefs. She tried hard to become like Rosgrana, Helen and Claire, a worthy member of the 'temple'.

But as she uncovered the sinister secrets of the temple, she realized she must escape . . .

Games . . .

A weekend in an isolated country house when the owner
is away seems like a great idea to teenagers Kirsty and
Genevieve. Patricia, invited along at the last moment, is
not so sure – especially when Kirsty asks her boyfriends
to join them for a party.

But the guests fail to arrive, the girls bicker and
boredom sets in. It seems there is nothing to do on a
bleak winter's night in the country after all. The house
has an intriguing past, however, and a seance – with
candle, wineglass and alphabet letters – might liven
things up. But what begins as a bit of fun soon gets out of
hand – and their foolish game plunges them into a night
of terror . . .

HEARD ABOUT THE PUFFIN CLUB?

. . . it's a way of finding out more about Puffin books and authors, of winning prizes (in competitions), sharing jokes, a secret code, and perhaps seeing your name in print! When you join you get a copy of our magazine, *Puffinalia,* sent to you four times a year, a badge and a membership book.

For details of subscription and an application form, send a stamped addressed envelope to:

The Australian Puffin Club
Penguin Books Australia Limited
PO Box 257
Ringwood
Victoria 3134